BECOME A[ ] W[ ]

This three-level reading ser[ ] beginning readers or impro~~ving readers and is based on~~ True and the Rainbow Kingdom episodes. The books feature common sight words used with limited grammar. Each book also offers a set number of targe[ ] [ ]ds are noted in bold print and are pr[ ] [ ]ry in order to reinforce meaning an[ ] [ ]y.

LEVEL 1 — LITTLE STAR

For pre-readers to read along

- 125-175 words
- Simple sentences
- Simple vocabulary and common sight words
- Picture dictionary teaching 6 target words

LEVEL 2 — RISING STAR

For beginning readers to read with support

- 175-250 words
- Longer sentences
- Limited vocabulary and more sight words
- Picture dictionary teaching 8 target words

LEVEL 3 — SUPER STAR

For improving readers to read on their own or with support

- 250-350 words
- Longer sentences and more complex grammar
- Varied vocabulary and less-common sight words
- Picture dictionary teaching 10 target words

CrackBoom! Books is an imprint of Chouette Publishing (1987) Inc.

Text: adaptation by Robin Bright of the animated series TRUE AND THE RAINBOW KINGDOM™/ᴹᶜ, produced by Guru Studio.
Original script written by Dave Dias
Original episode #102: Wishing Heart Hollow
All rights reserved.

Illustrations: © GURU STUDIO. All Rights Reserved.

Chouette Publishing would like to thank the Government of Canada and SODEC for their financial support.

Bibliothèque et Archives nationales du Québec and Library and Archives Canada cataloguing in publication
Title: The great cave rescue / Robin Bright; illustrations, Guru Animation Studio.
Names: Bright, Robin, 1966- author. | Guru Studio (Firm), illustrator.
Description: Series statement: True and the rainbow kingdom | Read with True. Level 2 (rising star)
Identifiers: Canadiana 20200084828 | ISBN 9782898022692 (softcover)
Classification: LCC PZ7.1.B75 Gr 2020 | DDC j813/.6—dc23

Legal deposit – Bibliothèque et Archives nationales du Québec, 2020.
Legal deposit – Library and Archives Canada, 2020.

Printed in Scott, Canada
10 9 8 7 6 5 4 3 2 1   CHO2105 JUL2020

READ WITH

True
and the
RAINBOW
KINGDOM

LEVEL
2
RISING
STAR

THE GREAT CAVE RESCUE

Adaptation from the animated series: Robin Bright
Illustrations: © GURU STUDIO. All Rights Reserved.

CRACKBOOM!

The Rainbow King is collecting Wishes inside a **cave**.

He finds plants that look very **thirsty**. They need **water**!

The King calls True for help.
The **cave** is **dark** and **spooky**.
To find the King, True will need
help too!

To the Wishing Tree!

True explains the problem to Zee.
"Let's sit and have a think,"
says Zee.

"Wishing Tree, Wishing Tree, please share your wonderful Wishes with me!"

What are True's three Wishes?

ELONGY can **stretch**.

WO GLO can make **light** that is very bright.

SQUIDZY can grab onto
anything.

Thank you, Wishing Tree!

In the **cave**, True and Zee must
cross a deep **pit**. They need
a bridge!

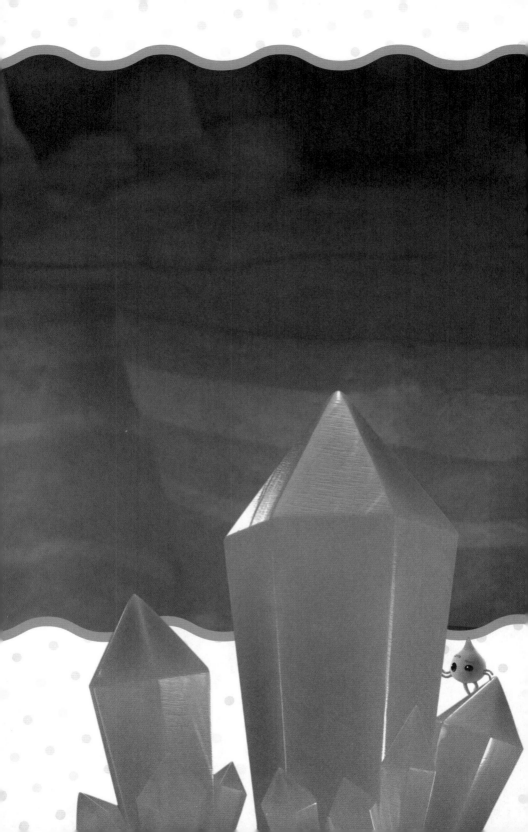

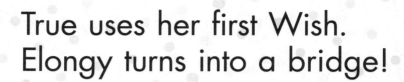

True uses her first Wish.
Elongy turns into a bridge!

The **cave** gets darker. Now
True and Zee need some **light**.
True uses her second Wish.

Wo Glo makes **light** so True and Zee can see. They find the plants.

Then they
find the King.
Hugs!

"Look how **thirsty** these plants are," the King says. "They get **water** from that small hole above. But it's not enough."

True calls her third Wish. Squidzy sticks to the roof of the **cave** and makes the small hole bigger. **Water** sprays out of the hole. The plants finally get what they need!

Outside the **cave**,
Bartleby has prepared a picnic.

"Thank you for helping me,"
the King says to True and Zee.
"You're welcome," says True.
"Friends always help friends!"

Picture Dictionary

cave

spooky

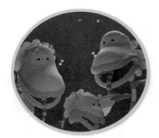

thirsty

water

dark

light

pit

stretch